THE AMISH DISAPPEARANCES

AN AMISH MYSTERY

By

PAIGE MILLIKIN

Copyright © 2017

Paige Millikin

INTRODUCTION

Nevada is a determined journalist who is after her first Pulitzer prize. When she learns about the disappearance of three different women outside Amish country she knows in her gut that something isn't exactly right in the quaint community. She has lost some of her faith throughout her own life, but when she meets a handsome carpenter he makes her question the real reason fate has pushed them together.

In writing this book, I wanted to examine the concepts of fate and faith, along with how life changes those ideals. Through Nevada's eyes we see both the best and worst of humanity. I hope this book is entertaining and stays with you long after the cover has been shut.

Blessings,

Paige

Paige Millikin

TABLE OF CONTENTS

Paige Millikin

LEGAL NOTES

Paige Millikin

CHAPTER 1.

"So, what do you think, Nevada? Do I have your buy-in on this piece? I'd hate to give it to another reporter given your history."

Nevada looked into the man's eyes, then down to the floor. She didn't like the prospect of travelling and she especially didn't like the idea of working on a story that involved any aspect of religion or faith. Nevada had turned away from that life long ago, and when she left her former church she didn't look back. She sighed and ran her hands through her long brown hair. Then she gnawed on her bottom lip, considering her options. Ned had been good to her through the years and had allowed her to get established in the community. After receiving her first assignment from him that landed her not only a front-page story, but a shot at the Pulitzer, she vowed her loyalty to him and that was a promise she didn't intend on breaking.

She exhaled and rolled her eyes. "Fine, Ned. Give me the file. Also, give me a few days to make arrangements. I don't really have family to worry about, but I do have my Schnauzer to consider."

"Good. I knew you'd see it my way, Nevada. That's the ace reporter I know. Now get out of whatever funk you've been in and find us a good lead on this one. I want us to win the big one."

Nevada chuckled and patted the bigger man on the shoulders as she took the file and walked out of his office. "Oh, Ned. You say that every time."

"Every time I mean it. Bring home the gold."

Walking back to her desk, she sat back in her office chair and stared at the manila folder that Ned had given her. Cracking it open, she began to read intensely hoping to find any clues to lead her in the right direction. After all, with every good story there were always two sides, often quite different. Somewhere in the middle though was the truth.

Nevada stared intently at the picture of the first missing woman; she was young and from her

The Amish Disappearances

photograph looked like the type of bubbly woman you'd expect to be answering phones at a physician's office. She was smiling and had bright blue eyes and wavy shoulder length blonde hair she wore in a fashionable style. Her name was Tabitha and she was married with two teenagers who attended a local high school in the area. Looking over the police reports it seemed out of character for Tabitha to just go up and missing. She was a pillar of the community, attending all the PTA meetings and volunteering her time on the weekends to whatever cause the local church was raising money for. Nevada found it curious that a woman with so many responsibilities would just vanish in the woods one evening with no explanation. Only her car was found on the outskirts of the Amish community on the edge of town.

The second missing woman looked decidedly different than Tabitha. Instead of having a boisterous smile and seemingly bubbly personality, she had an intense gaze in her photograph and wasn't smiling at all. She looked extremely focused. She had dark hair and dark eyes and wore a long t-shirt that was tie dyed. In her report, it stated that she was an independent contractor as an occupation, but some of her colleagues and associates reported that she had set up shop on a corner of town doing tarot card

11

readings and fortune-telling for cash. She looked to be one of those women, whose name you could never seem to remember with a face that was always familiar. Her actual name was Marie and despite the fact that she was obviously not traditionally career oriented her family said she was kind-hearted and wanted to stay out of trouble. She avoided the drug circuit and always made it home in time for dinner. She was the youngest victim who had just celebrated her twenty-first birthday. Her silver sedan was never found, but her cell phone's last known location was on the desolate road outside the Amish community.

The third known missing woman's name was Monica and she was a reporter for a local newspaper. She was covering for the paper's sportswriter who was ill and unable to attend an equestrian event in the area. Monica's friends knew that she would never leave a lead unturned and she always called to check in given the nature of her job. The was something familiar about the woman. She had blonde hair and looked spunky and bright. There was also a touch of sadness behind her eyes, which Nevada could only assume came after years of reporting. There were some stories that always haunted a reporter. Bearing witness to bloodshed and tragedy did tend to age reporters considerably and there were some crimes and stories that could never be wiped from someone's thoughts, no matter how much alcohol or other vices were consumed. Monica had gotten gas up the road in Allentown, but had not made it to the event. Her last phone call was right before the Amish community and then the signal went dead. The police were looking from this area all the way to the equestrian park 30 miles away for her car, which was never found.

Nevada felt a particular bond with Monica and vowed to find the missing woman. After all, that's how Ned got wind of the case to begin with. An old college buddy of his who was a copy editor for the paper contacted him since they were closer to the area to investigate the missing persons. One missing person would have gone unnoticed, but three in the past few months was a bit suspicious. The local and national media hadn't made a connection to the three disappearances, but to Nevada, all three being in such close proximity to the Amish community was very suspicious.

Nevada sighed and looked at the information in front of her. All the women were so vastly different in age, lifestyle, and occupation. They didn't seem to share any connections in the area, nor did they ever communicate with one another. It didn't seem like they had anything in common, but all three were led to the same stretch of highway outside the Amish community. Did they all just have some type of accident that just happened to leave them unable to call for help? Did all of them make some type of secret pact to disappear from their lives and vanish together? The latter seemed highly unlikely as they didn't travel in the same social circles, nor did they have any known contact with one another. Nevada had already checked their social media pages and they didn't have any mutual friends, nor did they have any groups in common they attended. Sighing, she flipped open her laptop and made herself some personal notes on the women, then she got on the internet and rented a car. It seemed as if the first step in finding the truth would be to take a road trip to see exactly where they were headed and determine if foul play could be involved. Nevada then picked up her phone and dialed Ned's extension. "Hey boss. You owe me for this one big time. I've rented a car and made arrangements for my pup. I'll be heading out of state in the morning."

"Sure thing. Just be sure to keep in contact while you're on your way and if you need back up or assistance, don't hesitate to get the authorities involved. You know the drill. Protect yourself first."

The following day, Nevada packed a duffel bag of clothes and prepared her messenger bag for her trip. Nevada did enjoy the travel she was lucky enough to do in her work. It seemed to calm the restless spirit within her, but at times she felt as if her apartment was not home, just merely a hotel she stayed at occasionally with her dog. Nevada was a bit of an oddity in the fact that she never really considered herself a people person. She was good at building a personal rapport with others and getting the information she needed from her sources, while making them feel comfortable. She didn't have many friends to speak of and she actually preferred it that way. She pulled open a drawer in the kitchen and then filled her silver, engraved flask. It was a present she bought herself when she celebrated her first Pulitzer nomination. The engraving simply read, "Truth." She found that it was appropriate because most people told their deepest truths when they were intoxicated, and she also had found quite a few truths about herself through the drink as well. Many weren't good.

Nevada mentally catalogued all of her supplies and found them to be in order. After stashing the flask in her messenger bag, she sat her bags by the door. She then walked into the kitchen and watered all her plants before she left. She had already taken her dog to the vet's office who had agreed to house him when she was on assignment. Nevada already missed his short, stubby wagging tail, perky ears, and soulful brown eyes. She always said that he picked her to be his human, it wasn't the other way around. He came to the edge of the cage at the local animal shelter and immediately began licking her finger. Since she was mostly a recluse when not working, he became her comfort after long nights on cases and always seemed to uplift her when she was feeling blue. His pepper gray coat gave him an old man, wise beyond his years look, which made him her number one confidant.

As Nevada made one last round through the apartment making sure that she turned off the lights and the coffee pot, she looked at her neatly made bed and tried to remember the last time she had a date. Grabbing her keys and her bags she locked up and walked downstairs to her rental car. She popped the trunk and put her bags in recalling the last time she did remember going out. Nevada had taken the time to pick out the perfect maroon colored dress. She stood in front of the mirror agonizing what side to part her hair on and the perfect shade of lipstick. Standing in her best pair of heels and looking the best she'd looked for quite some time, she then took a taxi cab to a restaurant where she sat alone at a table drinking water and waiting for a stranger she had been messaging on the internet. She agreed to meet him in a public place after messaging with the man for a few months off and on. His name was Marcus and he was a broker in an investment firm. He told her he hadn't dated much since losing his former wife to cancer. He was intelligent, funny, and seemed to know exactly all the right words to say to make her day better as he became a close friend.

When he arrived he looked nervous, yet he seemed happy to finally meet her in person. He was more handsome than what she envisioned. His short black hair had started to fade into silver streaks in spots and he was the perfect gentleman. He seemed genuinely interested in her career and found it fascinating that someone as young as she had already received her degree and was working in her chosen field. Nevada told him about her choice to pursue her education and passion over the opportunity to join her father's company as his partner. Nevada just never felt the life of a businesswoman calling her; instead she found true enjoyment unraveling mysteries and telling stories. Near the end of the evening, Marcus slid his hand across the table, and looked into Nevada's eyes deeply. He then placed his hand on top of her own and she blushed deeply. He looked down and smiled awkwardly, asking her if she wanted to date him on a regular basis.

She accepted his offer and found her weekends full of dinner dates and surprise tokens of affection. Marcus sent flowers to her office, and even took it upon himself to show up on occasion at her apartment to simply surprise her by cooking dinner, or bringing over a bottle of wine. Though they seemed like the perfect couple it didn't take long for Marcus to become distant. His phone calls became less frequent and when they were together he was almost constantly looking at his watch or just staring off into the distance, not really listening to Nevada's questions. After Nevada had turned down his advances late one night when he was attempting to become intimate, Marcus got sullen and didn't utter more than one word to her for the rest of the evening.

Nevada soon learned the heartbreaking truth about Marcus. She was determined to see if she could figure out why he had changed. He had seemed so interested in her at the beginning of their correspondence, and when they were together he was once a man who seemed to genuinely enjoy her companionship. She decided to look up his home number and call him at home late one night after attending an office party that Ned threw. Marcus had told her he couldn't attend because of work obligations. When a woman answered the phone, she was dumbstruck. He hadn't mentioned he had any siblings and his mother lived across the country. She questioned the woman on her identity and dropped the phone immediately bursting into tears. She chided herself for not seeing all the signs in the beginning and taking Marcus at his word. His entire identity as a grieving widower was a lie. He was married with children at home and never had a former wife. She was upset that her intuition was wrong about his character and she was left a heartbroken mess. Marcus had the audacity to try and explain himself, but Nevada was finished with him. She hadn't really pursued anyone since Marcus and at times wondered if there was indeed anyone on earth that was meant to be with her and her only.

Paige Millikin

CHAPTER 2.

Shaking off the thoughts of Marcus, Nevada began her trip down the interstate to the northern part of the state. She decided she would follow the same route that corresponded to each of the missing women's hometowns, so that at some point they would be travelling the same section of freeway. She put on her iPod and blared the loudest music possible to keep her alert during the drive and thought about what would possess three women to be in the same area, all from different walks of life. There were no known tourist destinations in the area and each of them had a reason to come home. They had loving families who were obviously missing them. As the skyline turned to a bright shade of pink, nearing dusk, she pulled over on the side of the road and made a phone call to Ned. She wanted to let him know exactly where she was in the event he needed her back at the office. She also knew the older man did tend to worry about his star reporter at times. She had learned this lesson early on in her career when she took an assignment then didn't check in. She was undercover investigating a ring of arsonists when she was unexpectedly arrested. Ned let her serve twenty-four hours, before coming to bail her out. She hadn't missed a check in point since that night.

Ned was really the only person she considered anything like family any longer. Never close, her parents had practically disowned her when she made the decision not to continue in the family business after high school, instead working odd jobs and waitressing to get her tuition money for college. She received her Bachelor's in journalism and began working for a small, local paper that mainly reported on the town's gossip with weekly editions. She found herself lost when it folded. Disheartened she went back to waitressing when she met a customer who changed her life. The elderly gentleman sat in the corner sipping coffee as he did every Saturday morning. Sometimes he would order pie or a croissant to go with his beverage. He wasn't like many of her other customers, who sat at their table or booths immediately pulling out their cell phones. He seemed content just sitting in silence and watching the people around him. She never forgot the conversation they had that gave her a renewed sense of purpose and changed her life. After most of the patrons had left the diner was quiet after the morning breakfast rush. He signaled for Nevada to come to his table. "How are doing Miss?"

"Well... I'll admit I'm tired today. I just had quite a few rude customers so I'm sorry I'm not my usual chipper self."

"I understand. There's no excuse for rudeness in my opinion. People these days are always in so much of a hurry. There's a certain kind of grace in patience if you ask me."

"Ha. Yes, I certainly agree with you. Can I get you a refill?"

"Please. Also, I'd appreciate it if you'd join me for a cup as well."

"I'm not really supposed to sit with the customers, but since my boss is away on a meeting, I'd be delighted to take my break now."

She returned with two fresh, steaming cups of coffee and sat across from the older gentleman. She closed her eyes for a moment, relieved to be off her aching feet. "I've been coming to this diner for almost a year now and every morning you bring me my coffee just how I like it, and it occurred to me I don't even know your name. I apologize for treating you as if you were a disposable person. So what's your name, Miss?"

"My name's Nevada."

"Well, that's a lovely name, and also quite unusual."

"Thank you. I'm pretty sure my parents were at the hippie phase of their lives when they named me. What's your name? I don't think you've ever told me."

"My name's Paul. I'm pretty sure my parents were in their hippie phase as well."

"That's funny. So, you're not like most people who come in here sitting on their phones and constantly distracted by some type of entertainment. What do you do?"

"Ah. I had a feeling you were going to ask me that. See, I've shunned the whole cell phone revolution. I feel it disconnects us from one another too much. I see the same thing, mothers refusing to pay attention to their children because they're on Pinterest, couples refusing to have true intimacy with one another because they're more interested in posting their pictures on social media, and no one actually having genuine conversation because they'd rather text. I digress though. I'm a retired police officer and now I enjoy a different kind of peace."

"Wow. I bet you've seen so much in your career. I'm not really a waitress you know, I'm a down on my luck journalist, who's just stuck between jobs."

Paul looked at her with his kind, blue eyes and gently touched her hand. "Well, I think it's time that you stopped worrying about it and let God take over that situation."

Nevada looked at him with a combination of awe and confusion. She had never really been a religious person and her parents weren't either. They were both very conservative and rational people, who needed facts and figures to survive. They didn't really place much stock in intuition or faith and relied on science and sound judgment to assist in their decisions. "What do you mean?"

"What I mean is, I'd be delighted if you'd pray with me."

The man bowed his head and said a few words in blessing, then asked for favor to be placed on

Nevada to find her true path in life. From that day forward, Nevada did find favor in her life. She landed the job working with Ned and started attending the local church. She held her faith in high regard until she covered a story which had exposed a sex scandal that shook her to her core.

The Amish Disappearances

Paige Millikin

CHAPTER 3.

Shaking off thoughts of her past, and opting to focus on the task at hand, Nevada pulled her rental car over next to a small run down shed that marked the turn off to the road that led to the Amish community. It was a desolate road with tall trees lining each side. Further down, she could make out a small house made of wood with a large front porch. Nevada walked down to the house. An older man in a rocking chair was positioned on the wide front porch. He was slightly rocking and humming a tune Nevada did not recognize. He eyed her suspiciously.

"Afternoon," Nevada called out to the man.

"Uh huh. You lost young lady." The man replied.

"No. I am looking for Esther King. I am scheduled to meet with her today. I'm Nevada," holding out her hand, Nevada waited for the man to shake. When it was evident the handshake was not forthcoming, Nevada continued, "I'm here to write an article on the craftsmanship of your furniture. This community produces some of the finest furniture in Pennsylvania and I want to do a feature article on how it is made.

The older man's face relaxed a bit. He shook his head replying, "That it is. We have several good men in town who work very hard at their craft. The good Lord gave them quite the skill to carry forth. I see you have a vehicle. You won't be needing that here. You can park it behind the shed. Esther is at the community center right now finishing supper preparations with the other women." He pointed to a large barn shaped building further down the road.

"Thank you kindly, Mr. ?"

"Elder. Elder Jackson." He nodded his head in dismissal.

Nevada wanted to ask him more questions about his viewpoint of the road, but took the cue that the conversation was over and made her way back to her car to repark and get her bags.

***

Walking into the community center, Nevada could feel the heads turn as she walked up to a group of women placing trays on a long table.

"Good afternoon. I am Nevada Plankton and I am looking for Ms. Esther King." A small woman with gray hair done up neatly under her kapp stepped forward amongst the group.

"Oh, good afternoon Nevada, we were expecting you." Reaching out, Esther grabbed both of Nevada's hands in her own. "I told your periodical editor that it was so fortunate you wanted to come this weekend. You see, we are a very tight knit community, but this is a special weekend where we gather together to have our meals in the community center until the first harvest day Monday next. It is our tradition to thank God for the blessing of the fruits of the Earth that provides sustenance for us throughout the year. It is also a blessing you will be able to join

31

us," she said the smile on her face shining through her words as well.

Esther proceeded to grab Nevada a plate as she introduced her to the many townsfolk who had started to trickle in for the evening meal. Nevada tried her best to make a mental note of many of the individuals she wanted to get to know a bit better. Esther sat with her and the group of women she had first met. They were all very curious about her job as a 'magazine journalist' and Nevada found it disconcerting to not be able to share the whole truth of her occupation with these seemingly well-meaning women.

"I feel very fortunate to be able to share a story regarding the quality of your furniture with our readers. There is very little known about the craftsmanship. I suppose you don't have too many English visitors stopping by?"

Esther shook her head, "No, that is quite true. We are a bit off the beaten path, you see. Of course, many of our goods are sold in the shops up in Allentown. My friend Ruth and her daughters can jam, preserves, cucumbers, olives, and many other delicious treats for the Englishers. But Allentown is about as far as they come for our goods. This is our home, and we don't want this to become a... what do you call it Nevada, a tourist trap?"

The other woman at the table laughed and Nevada joined in. "Oh, you certainly don't have to worry about that with this article. While I do want to concentrate on how it is made, for the selling aspect, I will certainly feature the shops in Allentown."

"Ah, yes, your editor explained as much. That was how the Elders agreed and put me in touch with your employer. He really does have the gift of words, and his penmanship is exquisite." Nevada inwardly laughed at the thought of Ned writing an actual letter instead of hammering away on his laptop. He really went all out to set this up.

"The Elders. I think I met one of them when I first arrived. An Elder Jackson?"

"Ah yes, oh bless his soul." Esther shook her head and crossed her hands as if she was saying a silent prayer. "He is a very respected member of our community. His whole family was."

"Was?"

"Well, is. It's just that he lost his wife last year. She was ill for a few years and it broke all our hearts at her passing. And then their daughter, Abigail. She left for rumspringa after her mother passed. She decided not to return and we are all so saddened for him."

"Oh my, that is terrible. I saw him by himself on the porch and I thought he was not particularly fond of the fact that I was there, but maybe also he had a lot on his mind."

"Yes, dear." Esther patted her hand. "He does have a lot on his mind. Actually, all the Elders do. They are in charge of making very important decisions as per God's plan for this community." She nodded to the table to Nevada's left. A group of men all in black sat enjoying their meal.

One Elder stood and walked over to their table. He was tall with a long, grey beard and piercing dark eyes. "Hello, miss. You must be the young woman I was contacted about regarding the article on our fine woodcrafters."

"Yes. My name's Nevada Plankton. Thank you so much for your hospitality. I very much appreciate you letting me observe this weekend. I wanted to come and see the community for myself. My boss thinks since primitives are the new wave of home interior designs, it would be beneficial to see how some crafts are actually handmade."

The Amish Disappearances

"Well, primitive is a word used for all things country now, but there is joy in our craftsmanship and hopefully you will see the full advantage of crafting things by hand as opposed to modern technologies. We have prepared a cabin for your stay. I dare say it is as rustic as our furniture. I'm afraid any electrical gadgets won't be of much use here. I'm assuming you're only staying the weekend?"

"Oh, more than likely. I won't be too big of a nuisance. You'll barely notice I'm here."

"I'm sure. Ah well, Esther, would you please show Miss Plankton to her cabin after you finish your supper. Goodnight, Miss. We rise early here in these parts, so if I were you I'd get some sleep."

Paige Millikin

CHAPTER 4.

Nevada opened the cabin door and looked around at her surroundings. Everything in the cabin was made from mostly wood, which she assumed had been cut and assembled on site. It amazed her to see that there were no modern conveniences, and it was deathly silent. She thought about Paul and smiled, thinking he would have liked it here; there was none of those cell phones to distract anyone in the community for certain. She used the flashlight on her own phone to locate an oil lamp which was in the center of the living room situated in the middle of a table. She lit the small flame and turned up the oil so the lamp would cast a bit more light in the room. She carried it around with her and lit as many lamps and candles she could find until the room didn't look as unsettled and didn't feel as empty and cold.

It didn't appear as if anyone had stayed in the room for quite a while and Nevada found this curious. She found it odd that people who focused so much on not wasting anything would leave a perfectly good structure unused. She thought the elder was peculiar, but she didn't really want to place a judgment on his character. It was her understanding that the very culture of the community was vastly different than portrayed on television and movies. She took a seat on a large, surprisingly plush sofa in the living room and sat her bags down beside her. She pulled out her camera and began taking some photographs of the cabin. She knew it was important to document every detail of her trip. She would repeat the process in the daylight as well, just to be sure that she had plenty of visual evidence to pour over when she returned to her office.

Nevada then decided to get a little more comfortable and took off her shoes. She didn't ascribe to many of the fashion rules that the women in her office did. Instead, she did most of her field work in jeans and sneakers. She attempted to dress up but always found when on assignment heels were cumbersome, especially when she literally had to chase down a lead. She pulled her legs up underneath her and took out her notebook. She began rolling the mystery around in her brain once more when she felt a noticeable chill. The temperature outside must have dropped considerably because her skin suddenly prickled with goosebumps. Sighing she stood up and looked around. Of course, there wasn't a modern source for heat in the cabin as the community didn't cater to guests with any amenities the rest of the community didn't have. She did however see a large crate of wood beside the fireplace readily available and a fire poker.

Lugging piece after piece of wood from the basket, she stacked them neatly and crisscrossed in the fireplace. She saw a long lighter that was situated on top of the mantle as well as a few shards of thinner strips she assumed were to be used for kindling. She placed them underneath and on top of the wood mound she built and lit the fire. The flames danced around her face and gave the entire room an unearthly, eerie glow. She crouched by the fireplace for a few moments, studying the pattern of the flames, making sure the kindling was positioned correctly to set the larger, thicker pieces of wood ablaze. When one of the logs finally caught, Nevada smiled in accomplishment. She never had the occasion to start her own fire before, but she was certainly proud of herself for succeeding. As the fire roared to life, she went back to the sofa and got comfortable once more. The heat felt good surrounding her body and despite being in a strange location without any modern conveniences she felt as if should could sleep soundly though the night. Nevada glanced at her camera once more and on a whim took a photograph of the roaring fire that she built in front of her. After all, she didn't quite know when she would have the opportunity to build one on assignment again. Despite the early hour she found herself yawning, maybe the lack of electricity and white noise had somehow forced her body and mind to relax. Perhaps without the constant onslaught of information she could let her mind have some peace and quiet. Maybe she was just exhausted from the long day and the drive. Whatever the case, Nevada found her eyes closing on their own while she reclined on the sofa. She gathered her bags, picked up an oil lamp, and wandered down a narrow hallway to what appeared to be a bedroom.

Nevada was no stranger to the dark, as she often did her investigative reporting in the dark, but there was something deeply disturbing about it this time. It was almost too dark. Perhaps it was the lack of any sound other than the steadily increasing drum of her own heartbeat in her eardrums as she opened the door. The heavy wooden door scraped against the frame and made a sick groan as it opened. She used her flashlight on her phone and the oil lamp to survey the room before stepping inside. It was very sparse, with minimal furnishings, save a dresser with a mirror which made her gasp when it caught the reflection of her light and a four-poster bed. She could tell by the layer of dust on the top comforter it had been a while since anyone had stayed in the room. She ran her hands over the blanket and as she reached the top of the bed was delighted to see there was also a fireplace in this room also. She sat the oil lamp down on the dresser and went about the same process as she did previously. She smiled at herself on how quickly she built the fire which not only knocked the chill out of the long vacant room, but also provided a bit of additional light, which comforted Nevada immensely.

She quickly retrieved her shoes and bag from the other room and then she unbuttoned her jeans and let them fall to the floor by the bed. She then pulled her form fitting t-shirt over her head and placed her hands behind her, unfastening her bra. She then quickly pulled another t-shirt out of her overnight bag and slipped it over her head. Nevada wasn't shy about her body in the least, but she preferred comfort over sexy any day, and her idea of lingerie was a long t-shirt without holes in it. She then pulled off the dusty quilt and stretched her tired body out overtop the cool, crisp white cotton sheet. She was surprised at the softness of the fabric. She was also surprised to find both the mattress and pillow supportive in all the right areas. As she felt the kinks being worked out of her back, her neck muscles relaxed as well. She somehow felt comforted even in the eerie darkness. As she drifted off, she wondered to herself if that was what faith was comprised of, simply feeling comforted in the black void of eternal sleep.

As Nevada slept, she began sweating; she would roll over and flip the pillow back over to the cooler side, press it to her face, then fall back asleep. When she would wake briefly though, she felt an odd sensation, like someone was in the room with her, watching or staring at her from the dark corner. Dismissing the feeling to being in a strange place, where there were unsettling events being unraveled in her brain, she thought nothing more of the feeling. Just as she drifted off and fell into a deep sleep for what seemed like hours, Nevada woke up cold to the core as the grandfather clock in the hallway began chiming. She screamed and sat up, immediately reaching for her cell phone to use as a flashlight. She trailed the beams all throughout the room and was relieved to discover she was alone. She padded quickly down the hallway in her socked clad feet and looked at the clock hands. They were not moving and the pendulum in the bottom of it didn't appear to have been moved in quite a long time because it, as well as other objects in the cabin had layers of dust stuck to various surfaces.

Her mouth dropped in horror at this discovery, but Nevada knew she had to keep a level head and that morning should bring some answers when she could investigate further in daylight. She took one last sweep with the light on the clock and noticed a shiny object laying on the bottom shelf of the clock. Nevada carefully opened the glass case, careful not to disturb the three large weights leading to an ornate wood carved pendulum held by dusty chains. Reaching for the object, she noticed it was actually some type of journal with a silver embalm on the cover that was shiny and clean compared to the gritty residue covering the rest of the book. Closing the case to the clock, she took the journal with her back to the bedroom and stretched out once more. Placing the journal up to her flashlight and snuggling under the comforting warmth of the blankets, she began to read.

"I'm so excited. I can't believe I'm actually here, ya know? So far this place is everything it was promised to be. I have found my new place in the world I think. I mean, after all, I've already reached the point in my life that I feel I can't do any more good works on the outside. My beloved children have turned into responsible adults with families of their own and my husband has turned into the type of man that is kind and secure in his future. I have affected them to the fullest extent possible. He was right. Sure, people may say 'Sally, you've lost your mind', but I know exactly what I'm doing. I'm starting over for the right reasons. When I met him I didn't realize how broken of a woman I was. I had already fulfilled the mission the Lord set before me on the outside world. Now I'm onto my true purpose."

Nevada was jolted awake by the words on the page. She had stumbled on what appeared to be a journal from a woman who left the English world to join the Amish. How did it get here? Did this cabin used to belong to this woman? She flipped to the next page which continued her narrative, but seemed later in Sally's stay. She unfortunately didn't date any of the pages. Nevada attempted to make sense of a few sentence fragments, and then found another page almost full near the back. "I don't think I have much longer, I just wanted to write this down in case someone finds it. Please tell my family I'm sorry. I didn't know coming here would be my demise. I was promised so many things, but it's so terrible here. He should not be revered, he should be feared. I don't remember the last time I slept. I know I ate last week because I was really full of grace, or so he told me. I miss my children, I know they're worried. I have made a mistake leaving them, now they will be motherless for the remainder of their adult lives. I was promised the path to true enlightenment and now I can't remember my name most days. I just know that I'm weak and can't go on much longer, not that I will have a choice in the matter. He was speaking to me today about the great purging of sinners. Then I remember his black eyes staring at me, almost boring a hole through my body. I'm next. If you're reading this leave while you can... it's not worth it. Don't let the true devil's disguise fool you. To my husband, thank you for your years of loyalty and dedication. You've become the man I always knew you could be. You're kind, honest, full of life and integrity. I don't want you to be lonely in your old age, so please remarry and make your new bride just as happy if not happier than you've made me in your golden years. Live and carry on with your lives. I'll be watching from a better place. I love you with all my being."

Nevada placed the journal in her bag and lay back in bed, turning off her flashlight as a tear ran down her face. Those were the last words Sally had written. She didn't know Sally's fate, but this wasn't a simple missing person's case any longer. Nevada knew in her gut that there was foul play involved in this community and wondered how many women there had been? She resolved herself to finding out the truth and honoring all of the women's memory. Nevada closed her eyes and forced herself to fall back asleep so she would be more focused the next day.

The Amish Disappearances

Paige Millikin

CHAPTER 5.

As the sun rose, Nevada awakened and wiped her blurry eyes. It came streaming through the cabin window and she could already hear community members outside tending to their chores. She pulled the pillow back over her face and closed her eyes once more trying to lull her body back to sleep, but it was to no avail. She rose slowly and got dressed in her typical jeans and t-shirt combo, then pulled on her socks and sneakers. Nevada then walked into the tiny bathroom and was at first baffled by lack of a sink. An old-fashioned tub sat in one corner and a toilet in another. Sighing, she was relieved the cabin had indoor plumbing, but no running water. A pitcher of water was found by the kitchen counter. She brushed her teeth then splashed some cold water on her face, which not only cleaned the oils from her pores, but made her feel revitalized and alert. She would need all the energy she could muster, because she was determined to find some answers and solve the mystery of what happened to the missing women.

Picking up her messenger bag, she flung it over her shoulder and opened up the cabin door into the bright morning. She squinted her eyes against the brightness and rubbed them to adjust. She then shut the door behind her and walked to the center of the town, seeing the men and women already up and working on their chores. She decided to start her questioning by asking a group of women hanging up laundry what if anything they knew about the missing women. Before she could reach them however, she was approached by the elder who approached her at the community hall the previous night. He had the same stoic expression as before, his eyes revealing nothing about his true feelings. She mused to herself that she was glad he would never be a poker player. "Morning, Miss Nevada. I trust you had a good night's sleep here. Feel free to observe anything in the community you choose, though I warn you we have breakfast early here so if you were hoping to eat anything before our late meal then I suggest you do it now. We share in all our meals here in the community building in the center of town for this special time leading up to Harvest. You should probably go now before the women start cleaning up."

"Okay. Thank you I'll do that. Esther mentioned the Harvest celebration. I am so honored to be able to be here during it. I don't think I mentioned this, but I really appreciate the hospitality. This place is so different than what I was expecting. And please, call me Nevada."

"Yes. I realize it must seem strange to you living your life on the outside with your modern technology. Here things are simpler, because we believe that by stripping away all distractions, we can truly find a direct path to the Lord. "

"I find that fascinating, I will have to meditate on that personally. Thank you again, I'll see you this evening?"

"Yes. I do hope you will consider attending our evening prayer session before supper. Something tells me that you were sent here for a very specific purpose."

"Oh, I think I most certainly was. Yes, I do think I will join you."

"Very well then, have an enjoyable day, Miss Nevada."

Paige Millikin

She turned and headed toward the community building to have some breakfast before spending the day speaking with the residents. Feeling as if she were being followed she turned around once more to see the older man walking away with no one behind her. As she walked to the dining hall though she couldn't help feel bit of unease when she inhaled and smelled the delicate floral scent of incense in the air. She knew one of the missing women was a fortune teller and more than likely used incense as a tool to convince her clients she was legit and correctly divining their futures.

Opening the door to the community center, she took the sights in more keenly than the afternoon prior. She saw rows of large, handmade tables and chairs lining the room. There was a buffet set up at the head of the room. A few women stood stirring large batches gravy and putting the trays of egg, bacon, biscuits, and sausage on the long table. Further down she saw stacks of pancakes and plenty of jarred honey and syrup. Nevada walked straight to the buffet and took a plate. The women looked at her, agape at her dress. They were not accustomed to serving outsiders breakfast. "Hi, good morning. How are you?"

One of the woman Nevada recognized from the previous day responded, "I think I can speak for all of us when I say we are well this morning, blessed by a full night's rest. Did you enjoy your stay here?"

"Oh. I certainly did. I don't think I've ever fallen asleep so easily. I suppose it was the quietness, or maybe the lack of text messages from my boss."

"Text messages?"

"It's a type of communication on a cell phone. Listen, I know I must look strange to you, but I'm hoping you can help me. Do you remember the last time you saw any women here dressed differently than yourselves?"

The woman scooped up some eggs and bacon, placing it on Nevada's plate then turned her eyes downward. She got quiet and looked over at the other woman beside her who chimed in as Nevada moved to her position on the buffet. "Occasionally we have guests like you, but it's only on rare occasions. You'll have to forgive my sister; she's not used to having visitors. I think you're the first outsider that she's encountered in quite some time. What brings you to visit our quaint community?"

Nevada smiled and nodded in appreciation, accepting the food the older woman offered, noting that she had not seen her yesterday. She then responded, "My boss sent me here on assignment. I'm a reporter. I'm researching living without modern conveniences and wanting to witness how some handmade goods are crafted for a feature story. I think it's marvelous how intricate and detailed some of this furniture is, without the use of modern technology to craft it."

"Oh my, yes. Our artisans here are among the best. Truly blessed by the Lord in their gift of creation. I think you'll find once you sample our cooking that you won't have the desire for anything processed again. I know that you young outsiders live on quick meals prepared from frozen synthetic meats, but here we take a certain pride in the things we grew and tended to with our own hands."

"Judging from the meal last night, I think you are certainly right. It smells amazing; when I approached the building my stomach started rumbling. I appreciate your kindness. I'll be sitting now."

She took her tray and walked to the center of the room where she spotted a young man sitting alone. He had honey colored blonde hair and was tan. She approached him and he smiled at her briefly, before returning his attention to his breakfast. "May I sit?"

"Certainly."

"Hi. My name's Nevada. What's your name?"

"My name's Stephen. It's nice to meet you."

"So, this smells delicious. Thank you for allowing me to sit with you. As you can see, I'm certainly not from around here. So Stephen, what do you do here?"

"I'm a carpenter. I built this table and chair you're sitting at. I don't see many outsiders here anymore. Why are you visiting?"

She ate a mouthful of eggs and sampled some bacon, then responded. "Wow. This is amazing. I could certainly get used to the food here. I'm here to write a story for a magazine. Actually, you are a key person I need to interview. It's a story on the art of handmade crafts for my boss." She smiled at him, looking into his sparkling blue eyes, "I think I just became a very lucky journalist."

"You may be, but I think we would have found our way to one another eventually today."

"What do you mean, Stephen?"

He finished his plate, and then ran a hand through his short blonde hair. He felt his heart begin to beat faster when she returned his gaze, and he knew that this attraction he felt for Nevada came from a higher source. "The Elders told me that you were coming this weekend. They wanted me to show you my shop. There are several craftsmen in town, but they thought you would be more comfortable speaking with me."

"Why would that be?"

"Well, I haven't been in this community long. I came from another Amish town and have spent some time in the English world. They thought I would be able to relate to you a bit more than the other men. What is the angle for your story?"

"I'm not sure what you mean?" A blush started to creep up Nevada's cheeks. Thinking about Esther's concern yesterday she quickly added, "I want to make it clear that I will not be trying to sell this community to come to for tourists." Inwardly she agreed that was the furthest from the truth. "I just want to highlight the craftsmanship and complexity of working without modern tools."

"Are you sure that is all? I was behind you in line up there. You weren't just asking about how a table is made. But, besides that, perhaps you are searching for enlightenment."

The Amish Disappearances

"Really? What makes you think I'm not enlightened?"

In an action that surprised even him, Stephen reached across the table and placed his hand over top of Nevada's. "Oh, I think you're much more than you appear. Still though, I've seen women like you here before. You don't think you're lacking anything at all, and then you come here and realize that you've been missing something in your life. You think you're in control, but really you're not, Nevada, and the sooner you realize that the better your life will be."

Nevada looked at him and once more felt pulled into his deep eyes. She didn't pull her hand away; she simply held to his tighter and responded, "You only think you now my life. You probably assume I'm nothing more than a lustful sinner who has forsaken the Lord and turned my back on religion because I live in the outside world. Isn't that right, everything in the outside world is tainted?"

"Not necessarily. There are good people in the outside community, just as there are sinners here. You see, Nevada, it's not one size fits all. I can tell that at some point you had a relationship with God. I'm just wondering what happened."

"You're awfully inquisitive to be a carpenter. You'd make a fine journalist one day."

"You're awfully lost to be a journalist. Maybe you'll find yourself one day."

With that remark, Nevada pulled her hand from his and blushed deeply. She didn't know why she was so drawn to this man, whom she should have been insulted by. She could tell, however, he came from a different place with the comment, it's wasn't meant to insult or injure. "Well, do you think you could do me a big favor and let me watch you work for a bit? I do have a story to write and I've only the weekend here in the community to get all the details."

"Sure, let's go Nevada. I'll show you just how beautiful something handmade can be."

They walked through the town square together and stopped when they got to his workshop. He opened the heavy wooden door and pulled open all the blinds, allowing the natural sunlight to stream through the openings. There were several piles of wood in the corner, which had already been planned and a few bigger logs that hadn't been treated or cut yet. The entire room smelled of sawdust and rich lacquer. She observed several saws hanging on the wall and a few larger saws and axes sitting on a large tool table as well. She did notice that he had a homemade blade sharpener and a table saw that had a hand crank on one side. He possessed all the tools that outside woodworkers used, it was just none of them were powered by any form of electricity.

"I am a bit old fashioned around here. There is another carpenter in the community who sells a lot of goods to the outside. He uses these tools but also has a diesel generator to power his air tools."

"Air tools?"

"A diesel generator is power connected to an air compressor which generates high pressured air to power tools such as a table or circular saw."

"I thought this community was pretty strict on the electricity rule?"

"It is. We are, but it is permitted to run generators. We just do not have any power source that is part of the outside electrical grid. I just get a lot of satisfaction from making things with my hands."

He pulled out an unfinished desk he had been working on for the church elder's new office. It already had the form of a solid piece of furniture, it just didn't have any detail nor had the components of a drawer yet. "So, what I'm doing now is I'm taking this piece I roughed out and I'm cutting a place out of the center for the drawer. You know, Nevada, making furniture can be a nice metaphor for life. Sometimes we have to really just rip out our insides to make something new and functional, don't we?"

"I'm curious to know what you've ripped out of who... that's some very strange talk, considering what's happened here, don't you think?"

"I'm sure I don't know what you're talking about, Nevada. I was merely discussing how important it is to shed our old skin before trying to get back on the path the Lord intended us to follow. So tell me, Nevada, do you trust me?"

The Amish Disappearances

Paige Millikin

CHAPTER 6.

She didn't respond to his inquiry, she just watched him work in silence, as he meticulously sawed and sanded until he was pleased with his progress on the drawer. Once he was satisfied with the fit of drawer in the frame, he took it out and moved it onto his workbench where he used clamps to hold the drawer in place while he hand bored holes in the center for a pull knob or handle. She studied his hands as he completed his work. They were calloused, yet steady. He moved slowly and relied on his shoulders for cuts that required more strength. After he finished sanding the drawer he moved it to another area to be prepared for varnish. "Can I ask you a question, Stephen?"

"Yes, but I do remember asking you one you didn't answer a few minutes ago. I will still answer yours openly and honestly though."

Nevada took her time forming her sentence, she didn't want to offend her new-found contact, yet she didn't want to blow her cover either. "Are you happy here in the community?"

"Yes, I should say I am. It's a very simple life I lead, but a spiritually fulfilling one. Why do you ask, do I appear unhappy?"

"No. It's not that at all, it's just..."

"Go on."

"I think the outside world could use a good man like you among its population."

"Well, I'm flattered for you saying so, but fate put me here and I assure you there are good men in the outside world as well."

"Stephen, can I ask you another question?"

"Only if you answer my first one."

"Yes... I'm slightly bothered to say this, but yes, I trust you."

The Amish Disappearances

"Why are you slightly bothered about it Nevada?"

"I normally don't trust people at all. I've learned that the majority of people are selfish and let their own greed and vices direct their actions. I've learned that it's a rare occurrence that people will do things purely out of kindness or love."

"Hmm. Maybe I can change your perspective concerning that during your stay here. Will you be so kind to hand me that brush that's in the corner?"

Nevada picked up the brush and handed it to him as he opened a metal can containing his varnish. She wrinkled her nose at the fumes as he popped off the metal lid and it made a loud clunk that broke their silence. He dipped the brush in the clear liquid and twirled it around the container several times; he took extra care to make sure that none of it hit the floor as he applied the first layer of the clear coat. "Why are you doing that?"

"Oh, this is just a clear coat. It will help prepare the wood for its new stain. It also helps seal any damage caused by sanding and provides a smooth finish so there are no splinters when it's polished."

"This is a rather involved process, isn't it?"

"Yes, but things that are worth it usually are."

"Where did you learn this craft?"

Sitting the sealed wooden drawer back on his work area, Stephen placed the lid carefully back on the metal can and gently tapped it down with his mallet. "My father. He was much more skilled than me though. Well, that's all I can do on this piece until the sealant dries. I certainly hope you saw enough for your article. I'm surprised you didn't take any photographs for the magazine. I know how important photos are now with articles, the young folk here in the community always ask for more pictures with their lessons rather than just words."

Nevada hesitated a moment then responded, "Yeah. Um… I think I have just enough. Your question before… yes. Yes, I trust you. I don't know why I trust you, but I do."

Stephen closed the gap between them and placed his hand on Nevada's shoulder. She normally would have flinched at the contact, or at least taken a step back, but she was motionless at his touch. She was calm somehow. "Nevada, I'm glad you trust me. So, can I ask you a question now?"

"Sure."

"Please, tell me what you are really writing about."

Nevada furrowed her brow and shook her head in confusion at Stephen's question. "I'm not sure what you're talking about. I told you, it's an article on your craftsmanship."

"That you haven't taken any pictures of or asked any in-depth questions on. Tell me, are you staying in the cabin by the lake?" Nevada nodded. "Have you heard or seen anything that has bothered you?"

"What do you mean by that?"

"I just want to make sure you keep an eye on your surrounding while you are here. And be careful who hears you asking questions."

"You know, don't you? You know about the missing women."

"Yes, everyone here does. The police have been out and have spoken to many of us about the missing women. People are upset. When I moved here, there had already been a woman missing near here. I heard a lot about it pretty quickly."

"Oh. You came after the investigation started?" That made Nevada feel better about the blind trust she had placed in Stephen which went against her hardened heart.

Before they had a moment to finish their conversation, there was a loud rapping on Stephen's workshop door. It was Elder Hancock, another one of the high-ranking elders in the community, "Hello there Stephen, how are things going today?"

He was a wiry man who wore wire rimmed spectacles. He shifted his weight from one foot to another as he talked, and seemed to carry nervous energy with him like a badge of honor. He immediately reminded Nevada of Ichabod Crane in both gesture and appearance. Stephen didn't react to the anxious energy that Elder Hancock put forth; he remained calm with a neutral expression on his face as he replied. "They're going well today Elder. The Lord hath provided me with ample sunlight to do my work. Woodworking is always easier when it is sunny and dry outdoors. There's less swelling to worry about."

"Ah. That's very nice then, Stephen. I just wanted to check and make certain our visitor wasn't slowing down your progress. Elder Jackson wanted me to make sure she was getting exactly what she needed for her story. He also wanted me to remind her that lunch will be served in the community center in the next twenty minutes, so she should be going."

"Oh. Of course. Yes, we're getting along just fine, and I've actually got a very strong start to my day. The desk I've been working on is almost finished."

"Glad to hear it. Miss… Nevada, isn't it?"

"Yes."

"Can I escort you to lunch now?"

Nevada hesitated for a moment and met Stephen's eyes. She detected a subtle nod from him and decided to play along. After all, she couldn't blow her cover then no one would ever find out the truth about the missing women. "Oh, yes! Absolutely. Thank you so much for walking with me, I appreciate it."

Nevada nodded at Stephen and gave him a wink that remained undetected by Elder Hancock. She grasped onto Elder Hancock's proffered elbow and they wandered off together, taking their time strolling through the midday sun, chatting about the weather and her faux fascination with handmade furniture.

Paige Millikin

CHAPTER 7.

As Nevada and Elder Hancock walked through the doors of the community center she noticed Elder Jackson sitting at the head of a table full of older men with long beards, most of them greying. They bowed their heads for a few moments in what appeared to be grace before all picking at their trays. They smiled and laughed, seeming to enjoy their afternoon break. She nodded and smiled, occasionally chiming in and contributing to the one-sided conversation that Elder Hancock was having with her concerning the many vices of the outside world and how they led to society being doomed. They received their lunch, which as with breakfast smelled delicious and reminded

Nevada that she needed to keep up her strength as her stomach grumbled. The pair then walked to the table full of the elderly gentlemen and Elder Hancock asked permission for both of them to sit.

They were granted the privilege and all were very curious as to how Nevada liked their quaint community so far. The inquired also on how her article was coming along and she responded that she indeed had learned some valuable information while observing Stephen's carpentry earlier in the morning and the elders as a whole seemed pleased. As their conversation died down and the excitement of her arrival diminished, Nevada decided to see if she could get some more information on the real reason she was staying in the community. "So, I find this place absolutely charming. It seems like its own kind of paradise here. Honestly, I was surprised to find out just how smoothly things seem to run. It's not like it is in the city. There's no petty arguments, no random acts of violence, and it seems like everyone genuinely wants what's best for others. I don't think that could ever happen where I'm from."

Elder Jackson spoke up and responded, "Yes. You would certainly be surprised just how wholesome and wonderful life can be. You see, Nevada, everyone who's in this community has vowed to live their lives within the Lord, so there's no need for the vices which plague the outside world. Everyone here is equal and everyone has enough to live on and contributes equally, so greed is eliminated, hence there's no theft. The same thing goes for violence. We do not offend one another with callous words or actions that incite anger so there is no need for retaliation. If there is a grievance on one party's part, the issue is brought to our council to find what is fit and fair for both claimant and defendant. This eliminates violence almost entirely. Still, of course, boys will be boys and there's sometimes a schoolboy squabble, but sound parenting often curbs that before it's an issue to be brought within the church."

"What exactly do you mean by 'sound parenting'?"

"I'll use the shortened version of the verse that is most commonly equated with the situation. You know, Nevada 'spare the rod and spoil the child.' That doesn't happen here. Punishments are swift and stern, but most of our youth turn out to be fine, upstanding citizens going on to flourish in the community."

"Hmm... so far you've mentioned greed and violence. What about lust? That's another vice, another of the 'deadly sins,' if you will. How has your society managed to stop that?"

The table grew still and the air seemed to even quiet around the pair. Elder Jackson locked his eyes with Nevada's and gave her a steely glare. She knew she just struck a nerve within the older man. He didn't seem like he was going to back down, but Nevada didn't plan to either. His lips suddenly upturned in what Nevada classified as a cold smile. There was no warmth in the action, he was simply going through the motions to make sure the other elders didn't notice how shaken he actually was. "Hah! That is a very good question, Nevada, and I'm glad you brought it up. I applaud you for your natural curiosity; I would be asking the same questions if I were in your position, looking at what appears to be a perfect society. Of course, you would want to emulate it on the outside, but frankly there is too much corruption beyond these fences for it to ever happen."

"I understand that partially, but it really didn't answer my question. How does your society deal with the issue of lust and vice? That has been starting wars and has been the motivation for crime for a very long time. The fact is, if I remember correctly, ever since the beginning of our creation."

"Well, the issue itself is at the root of all evil, as are the other things, we've discussed. As a whole, evil itself cannot be eliminated, but we must make a conscious effort every day to be devout in our prayers and have faith. So to answer your question, we all know here it exists and have set up some stringent rules for being within the community. A vow of celibacy until marriage is one of those, and we also have a lengthy process for courtship."

"So, what if someone breaks those rules? Is that as simple as 'spare the rod'?'"

"Oh no, it's much different. As an adult, one is quite aware of their body and their actions and must devote themselves to the act of being pure in the Lord. If not, the punishment is excommunication. It's a simple punishment too, but in terms of what one stands to lose is much more severe. Can you imagine being separated from your family and friends, anyone and everything you hold close to your heart for the remainder of your existence? I certainly wouldn't want to even fathom it."

"No, I certainly wouldn't."

Feeling anger flood her body thinking about the missing women, who were separated now from everything they ever loved, Nevada stood up and exhaled. "Well, I certainly appreciate the nice lunch and wonderful conversation, but I would like to go ahead and retire to the cabin and get an early jump on my article, while the information is still fresh in my mind. Will you excuse me?"

"Certainly Nevada, it was a pleasure having that discussion with you. I'm glad you found it enlightening."

On the way back to the cabin, Nevada stopped by Stephen's woodworking shop and noticed he wasn't anywhere on site. His only work was the same piece they had started earlier in the day. She found it peculiar, and took out her notebook, quickly scrawling a note for him to meet her as soon as possible at the cabin. She knew that something was not right in the community and thought that he could help her find the missing women, or at least justice for them. She placed the handwritten note inside the desk drawer that Stephen was working on; hoping no one else would find it before he returned. She then walked back to the cabin, running the events of the past couple days through her brain. The facts were clear. At least three women disappeared; all were last seen on the highway leading to the community, where their trail just stopped. She found Sally's journal, which had mysteriously appeared and had shards of information showing there was something untoward inside the community. It implied that she was victim to at least starvation and sleep deprivation from what she could gather. She shut her eyes tightly, shaking off thoughts of other torture she must have experienced. She did have some eerie experiences the first night in the cabin, which she still didn't have a rational explanation for.

She quickened her pace and arriving at her cabin, shut the heavy door behind her, taking care to latch the hook. She found that peculiar as well. She didn't recall seeing a lock on any of the other building doors she had visited. She pulled out her cell phone and powered it on. It flickered and the screen came to life. She frowned as the low battery indicator light flashed. She had hoped her phone would have held a better charge, but using the phone as a flashlight seemed to have drained her fully charged battery. She tried to text Ned to check in, but she did not have any signal.

Grabbing her keys, she decided to hike back out to her car, thinking the signal would be better on the main road. She started the hike and started to job when she noticed the sun starting to slip over the horizon. Her attention on the horizon, Nevada tripped on the earth. She looked more closely at what she fell over and noted what appeared to be tire marks deeply engraved in the soil. They led off the path and Nevada decided to follow. She was still on Amish land and she knew from Elder Jackson that cars were not permitted here. The tracks led to a barn, made of partially rotted wood, but the doors chained together did not allow her admittance. She peered through a dusty window and saw a silver Chevy impala sedan. Knowing this was the same make and model as Marie was driving, Nevada became excited at the first piece of real evidence she had located. At the same time, her phone beeped noting that the power was completely out and it was shutting down. Before darkness completely engulfed her, Nevada started to jog back to her cabin. She had hoped to conserve enough battery to make an emergency phone call, should the need arise, but it didn't look like that was going to be the case. She passed by Elder Jackson's home. It was dark inside, but Nevada noted that the rocking chair was moving slightly, as if someone had just been sitting there. She got the feeling that someone was watching her. Not from Elder Jackson's house, but from behind her on the road to the barn. Nevada decided then and there to go to her car and drive to the nearest town to call Ned, and probably the police at this point. She reached into her pocket to grab her keys, but they weren't there. Nevada frantically searched all her pockets and realized that when she fell they must have slipped out of her pocket.

Without her cell phone's flashlight feature, Nevada knew she had no hope of finding her keys as

The Amish Disappearances

all sunlight disappeared from the sky. She decided to run back to the cabin where she could lock herself in till morning.

Paige Millikin

CHAPTER 8.

With the aid of the gas lamp, Nevada began scribbling in her own notebook. Letting the words out to make sense of what was going on in this community. She wanted to leave so badly, and had never felt a sense of foreboding danger like this before. She felt a chill creep upon her, so she duplicated the process she did the previous night, making fires in both the living room and bedroom of the cabin. As the fires roared and put off comforting waves of heat, she passed by the hallway window on her way to wash up for the evening. She caught a glimpse of movement out of the corner of her eye, and as she turned to follow it, she saw a figure passing by the window at the side of the cabin. She followed the dark figure, which quickly made their way across to the front of the cabin and making a loud rapping on the front door.

She flipped up the latch and Stephen came rushing in, hastily latching the door behind him, soaked in sweat. He seemed panicked and concerned. "I've been looking for you all day, I'm so glad you're still here." At that point, he noticed Nevada's terrified face. "What happened?!'

Unable to form a coherent sentence, Nevada flung her arms around him and sobbed into Stephen's chest. In all of her days as a reporter, she had never felt so out of her league, so terrified. He rubbed her back in soft motions, attempting to console her. "It's okay. I'm here now. You're fine. We're both going to be fine."

"I found a car. The same one the missing woman, Marie, drove."

"Where?"

"The barn, off the main road but set back quite a way. Near Elder Jackson's home."

"Elder Jackson? Did he see you? Did anything happen?"

"No, I ran straight back here. I don't know if he saw me, but, yes, I think he might have. Stephen, there's something I have to tell you, and please don't

82

tell another soul here, or it could spell my end. Do you understand?"

He nodded emphatically and Nevada continued, "Stephen, I'm not who you think I am. I am a journalist, but I'm not here to write a feature story on carpentry. I'm investigating the missing person's case, well three actually. It looks though as if there's been foul play involved. I have to get to the bottom of this before my time is up, or my identity is discovered."

"I know what you mean."

Paige Millikin

CHAPTER 9.

Before Stephen could reply, the door to the cabin was abruptly kicked open. In the doorway stood Elder Jackson. In the light of the glowing fireplace, he looked unnatural and ghastly, his face contorted in anger and rage. "That will be quite enough, Stephen. This is a private matter and it will be settled in the community, just as we have always settled our own affairs."

His voice was ice cold and he took several calculated steps toward them, carrying an axe. Of course, firearms were not permitted in the community, so it appeared he had found a different weapon of choice. He swung wildly, the axe hitting Stephen with the handle knocking him backwards. Nevada cried out to him, but he did not respond. The older man didn't waste any time in taking his first swing at Nevada, as she deftly dodged the axe. It landed in the side of the wood counter and made a heavy clunk as it embedded itself in the wood. Had he actually connected, he would have easily halved the wispy woman. He was much stronger that what he appeared and pulled the axe out in one easy motion. He then lunged at Nevada once more. In a defensive motion, she grabbed a glass from the counter and flung it at the man, sending shards all over the cabin. Undeterred she heard the glass crunch under his boots as he continued his pursuit. "Earlier you were asking about punishments, Nevada. Well, I think you know what the punishment for liars will be. It's right here in my hands. Why don't you make this easier on both of us and just admit you're living a life of sin and need me to purify you?"

"Is that what you did to those women? Is murder your way of purifying them? Is this your sick way of making society a better place?"

"Oh no. Ha. You really have it all wrong. I have created the perfect society here. See, here I am God. Things run smoothly because my congregation obeys me. Those women... well, I use the term loosely, they were a poor excuse for what a true woman should be. They were sinful, just like my girl,

The Amish Disappearances

Abigail. They were obnoxious, and they disobeyed all commands, and were not subservient in the least. Oh, I wish you could have been there, Nevada. Breaking them down, now that was a beautiful experience. In the end, they all saw the light. Each and every one of them cried to the heavens before I took them. My daughter, she left me. Her mother died and she left. They are both dead to me. Just like those women. Surely you see there was no choice. Just like there is no choice with you."

"Not in a million years. You'll never break me, you'll have to kill me first, and I will never utter your name over the Lord's. "

He lunged at Nevada with his axe once more, and she screamed out in pain as the sharp blade connected with the side of her leg. She fell to the ground immediately in pain. While Elder Jackson was solely preoccupied with Nevada, Stephen crept up behind him and struck him hard in the back of the head with the fireplace poker he had managed to obtain while the older man was distracted.

Rushing over to Nevada's side, Stephen held her in his arms, examining the wound on her leg, which was leaving blood to pool and stain the wood on the cabin floor. "You're okay. You're okay,

Paige Millikin

Nevada, we're going to get you some help, hang in there …my back up will be on the way shortly."

Stephen took off his jacket and ripped the sleeve at the seams, he then tied it around her leg using it as a tourniquet to stop the bleeding. "Stephen…what do you mean, your backup?"

Stephen looked into Nevada's questioning eyes and held her to him for a few moments, letting himself relax in the comfort of knowing she would be okay and the blade had not struck an artery. "I'm sorry I didn't tell you this sooner, Nevada… I couldn't risk it. I have been working this case for quite some time now. I know you mentioned three women, but unfortunately, they weren't Elder Jackson's first victims. Over the past year, there were five disappearances in this area. We never had enough information to specifically tie the Amish community. The coincidence that the women had been so close to the community did not go unnoticed. I've been undercover here for the last couple months."

"I don't understand, you mean you're not a mild-mannered carpenter?"

"Mild-mannered? Absolutely. I suppose now I'm a carpenter only through hard work and practice. I ran into Esther after lunch. I have been trying to make headway with the community members, but it has been difficult. They haven't opened up to me, but when I asked Esther about you she shared that she was worried about you. She would never accuse Elder Jackson, but she implied at lunch there were words between you too. She didn't like the way he looked or spoke. I was trying to find you. You weren't in your cabin or anywhere and I thought you had disappeared like the others. When I couldn't find you, I decided to call in for back up. I had been suspicious of Elder Jackson for a while and I didn't want you to be in danger while we proved his involvement. But, had it not been for you uncovering the evidence and provoking the Elder, we may not have had enough evidence to try him. With your testimony though, we can be sure that he faces justice when he awakens.

"The people here. They have been torn to pieces about these missing women. This is a good community. It will be hard for them to understand, but with the Lord's help, they will come to terms with this."

"How do you think they will be able to do that after the horrible things that happened?"

"Simple. They are strong together and in their faith. I think that the Lord gave us free will so that we could know what love truly is. Unfortunately, to know love means we have to have the context of hate and evil, which is where Elder Jackson lies in my book. I don't know if he had some kind of break when his wife died and his daughter abandoned him or if he was just pure evil. But we have to trust God and his plan. I believe with every fiber of my being he brings people together when they need to be joined."

She looked at Stephen who reddened at the comment as he stroked her cheek. She couldn't deny her own feelings for the handsome man any longer. As she looked into his deep blue eyes, she allowed herself to fall into a deep kiss, not questioning his motives, or morals, simply trusting in his strength.

"You know what Stephen, I think you're right. I think that's what true trust is."

Stephen placed a protective arm around Nevada's shoulder as he led her out of the cabin.

The Amish Disappearances

Paige Millikin

EPILOGUE

Nevada closed her laptop and picked up her now tepid cup of coffee. She had worked for the last two weeks piecing together all the missing parts to the story and had finally polished off the final copy and sent it to Ned.

What she had learned disturbed her to the core. Elder Jackson had been a respected member of the community and had lived there his entire life. No one had suspected him of the disappearances of the women, but there were some concerns of his mental health since his wife became gravely ill. His decisions on the council had been erratic and he disparaged women in the community where he had never spoken ill of anyone before. The community had been very forthcoming with their information, wishing transparency to uncover the sins of Elder Jackson so the victim's families could learn the truth. Elder Jackson himself had given the police a lot of information, including the whereabouts of the remains of the five missing women. The position of his home on the only road into the community and not in sight of the other residences was fortuitous for his evil doings. Since Elder Jackson had given a full confession, Stephen had allowed Marie to listen to the tapes of his interviews, which greatly assisted her story.

The first victim had been Sally Mitchell. She was a Caucasian woman from Philadelphia in her 50s looking for something more of her life and wanting to join the Amish community. She hadn't told her family much more than that, so when she was reported missing, there was not a lot to go on. Elder Jackson told the police that he had allowed her to come to the community, but soon realized that she was as "tainted" as his daughter who recently decided not to rejoin the community after rumspringa. He did not want the other community members to succumb to her lustful ways. At first, he barred her from leaving the cabin; the same cabin Nevada had been in. He then realized that was not going to hold her and brought her to his cabin where he had strangled her. He told the community that she had a change of heart and went home. They found Sally's remains with the others behind the barn that held Marie's car as well as two other dismantled cars.

The second victim was Sarah Washington. She was a sixty-year-old widow from Allentown who had befriended Elder Jackson's wife when she went to her shop to deliver canned jams and honey. Sarah had paid Elder Jackson a visit to see how he was coping with the loss of his wife and had brought him a prepared meal. Elder Jackson showed no remorse while he described killing Sarah for the fact that she must be a sinful woman for paying a man a visit in his home without the accompaniment of a male relative. He blamed her English ways of corrupting his daughter, who went with her mother often to the shop in Allentown.

Tabitha was the third victim. As suspected, her car had broken down at the top of the road leading to the Amish community. Elder Jackson's home was the first house she came to and he said that she was not worthy of their help. He had the least to say about Tabitha, not knowing anything about her life or who she was. He said that he strangled her with a rope and buried her out back.

The silver sedan did in fact belong to 21-year-old Marie. She was lost trying to get to a specialty herbal shop in Allentown. Elder Jackson was the first home she saw on the desolate road and she had pulled right up to it. Elder Jackson still expressed rage over Marie in her "slutty" English clothing with heavy make-up on. He spat his words out as he described her driving a car onto Amish land. He had used an axe on Marie and Nevada trembled as Elder Jackson relished the details of her death.

The final victim, not counting Nevada, was Monica. The reporter was on her way to the equestrian event when she too had car trouble. With her cell phone dead, she had walked to Elder Jackson's home. She looked in the window before knocking and saw Elder Jackson sitting at his kitchen table looking through a woman's purse. He caught her stare and quickly opened the door. Elder Jackson said that she was asking him questions that he did not like and when he found out she was a reporter, decided that she knew too much and was there to take him down. The police knew that her assignment had in fact been the equestrian event, but later interviews of her colleagues showed that she was curious about the disappearances near the Amish community and was informally looking into matters. The police surmised that the 'car trouble' may have been a ploy to check out the Amish community on her way to the real job she was assigned to. The irony of the fact that she had stumbled onto the real killer was not lost on Nevada.

She wondered how she even survived the first day with meeting Elder Jackson on the road, but surmised that he knew she was coming as did the other council members. Regardless, the safety of her presence being known did not last long. Elder Jackson vividly described in the tapes that he was "not finished with the Lord's work" and that Nevada needed to be placed in his mercy.

Stephen was the silver lining of the whole ordeal. The county Sherriff's Department he worked for was stationed in the city and his apartment was only five blocks from hers. They had seen each other daily since they both returned from the Amish community. Stephen was the break that Nevada needed as she poured over the materials for her story. Together, they rarely spoke of what happened, preferring to concentrate on getting to know one another and the promise of what was yet to come.

Read on for an excerpt of *Becoming Amish* by Paige Millikin.

Paige Millikin

The Amish Disappearances

BECOMING AMISH

By

PAIGE MILLIKIN

Copyright © 2017

Paige Millikin

CHAPTER ONE.

Beth perused the magazines, only vaguely hearing the sirens pass in the background. Her weekly grocery shop was almost completed and she was looking forward to a quiet evening back at home. This week had been a hard one at work, and she was in desperate need of some solitude. Her boss had been particularly mean, almost deliberately picking on Beth for no other reason than he felt like it. Heaving a sigh, Beth picked up a crossword magazine, wondering if she would have the time or the inclination to do it later. Opting instead for a Home Décor magazine, she brought her groceries to the checkout, frowning slightly as, through the store window, she saw yet another fire truck tear its way down the road.

"Thank you," she murmured, gathering her goods and taking them out to her car. The slight smell of smoke was in the air, and she silently prayed that, wherever the fire was, nobody would be injured. Sliding into the front car seat, she turned on the ignition and headed for home.

Paige Millikin

Turning the corner that led to her home, Beth pressed the brake, hard, slamming the car to a stop in the middle of the road. All she could see in front of her were red and white vehicles, an ambulance, and a crowd of people, all standing nearby, trying to see what was going on. "Please don't let it be me," she whispered silently, revving the car engine and moving it onto the side of the road. There was no way she could park any further up the road, given what was going on.

Getting out, she locked the car before taking a few, hesitant steps, into the gathered crowd. Her heart was pounding, her mouth growing dry as she walked further and further into the crowd. The acrid smell of smoke began to fill her lungs, and she could hear the dull roar of a blazing furnace. The further she walked, the more the dreaded realization of what she was about to see set in. Her house was the last on this street before you got to the Amish community, and, had it been the Amish, they would have dealt with it themselves. Pushing her way through the crowd, she suddenly stopped short, her hand going to her mouth. There, in front of her, was the remains of her home.

******

The Amish Disappearances

"Ma'am? Ma'am? Are you all right?"

The woman in front of him was swaying on her feet, her green eyes widening as she stared at the burning building. Her long blonde hair was tumbling all around her face, in stark contrast to the whiteness of her face. She was shaking all over, and, with a shriek, stepped forward just as the house began to crumble to the ground.

"You can't go near there!" Michael cried, catching her in his strong arms. "I'm sorry, ma'am!"

"You don't understand," Beth yelled, tension filling her. "That's my house! My home! Everything I have – oh! Whiskers!" She turned terror-filled eyes onto him, her hands moving up to cover her mouth. "Whiskers," she whispered again, her entire body shaking uncontrollably.

Michael realized that this must be the owner of the house, and, given what she was saying, must have a cat of some kind. "We managed to retrieve some things," he said, quietly, still holding her tightly. "Someone might have found your cat. Why don't we go and see?"

Beth could say nothing, allowing the stranger to lead her over to where a few men and some women were standing, each staring at the charred remains of what had once been Beth's home. From the looks of them, they were from the Amish community.

"Has anyone found a cat?" Michael asked, searching their faces. "This is the owner of the house. She says she has a cat."

"Oh, my dear!" An older woman stepped forward, taking Beth's hands and helping her to sit on the grass, with Michael gently easing her down. "You sit right here now and don't worry about your cat. Someone has him if I remember rightly. They'll have taken him back to the house."

Beth stared at her, hardly daring to believe that, in the midst of all the chaos, someone had found the only precious thing she had in life – her cat. "Ginger, with a white stripe running down the middle of his face?"

Pausing for a moment, the older lady thought hard, then smiled. "Yes, I think that's right. Quite a scratcher, that one! Didn't like to be held!"

"No, he doesn't," Beth whispered, relief flooding her. Her gaze moved back to her house, watching as the firefighters did their work. "There's nothing left." Despair wrapped itself around her, even though the older woman tried her best to buoy her spirits.

The Amish Disappearances

"There are a few things left," she said, patting Beth's hand. "They all got taken to my house, just since it's closer. We thought it best that they were kept safe. I'm Claudia, by the way. Now don't you worry, we'll take care of you."

Beth knew she should thank her, but couldn't find the words. Everything she owned, loved and treasured had been in that house, and now it was lying, literally, in pieces at her feet. Whilst she was relieved to know that Whiskers was safe, the knowledge that most of her possessions were gone was weighing down on her, to the point that she wasn't quite sure what to do. Too many thoughts were pouring in on her at all sides. *Where are you going to sleep now? What are you going to eat? How much will it cost to rebuild the house? Where will you get the money from? Who can you ask for help? How much do builders cost? Will my insurance cover it?*

"Miss?"

Pulled from her thoughts, Beth stared up at the firefighter who was walking towards them, a grim look on his face. "Y-yes?"

"This your property?"

Beth nodded, unable to pull her gaze from his face. His expression told her that the news would not be good.

"I'm sorry to say that this house is now completely unstable and will need to be razed to the ground."

A pale sheen covered Beth's face, as Claudia put a comforting arm around her shoulders.

"You'll have to rebuild."

Beth couldn't make sense of what he was saying, simply staring at him with her mouth agape.

Claudia, seeing her reaction, took over. "How did the fire start, may I ask?"

Turning his attention to her, the firefighter shook his head. "Seems there was some kind of electrical fault. You're not the only house to have been hit, but it was the only one to get this bad." Gesturing to the now smoking remains, he crouched down at looked Beth directly in the face. "Have you got somewhere to stay, miss? You'll have a few things to get sorted before you can even think about rebuilding. Family? Friends?"

"No," Beth replied, in a small voice. "I don't have anyone." No friends to speak of, given how much everyone just kept their heads down at work. There was no time for socializing, no time for friendship. Not when the wrath of their boss, Frank, was always something to contend with. He would always put a stop to any kind of social conversation. "What am I going to do?" she whispered, half to herself.

"You can come stay with us," Claudia declared, pulling her grip a little tighter around Beth's shoulders. "Ever since my oldest got married, we have a spare room and you are more than welcome to stay there. My youngest daughter is on *rumspringa* and we hardly ever see her either, so there is more than enough room."

Normally, the thought of living with the Amish would have caused Beth either to laugh or feel completely terrified, but right now, she felt nothing. She was numb.

"You'll stay with us," Claudia said again, as the firefighter walked away. "We'll be glad to have you."

If you would like to read more of Becoming Amish, please visit https://www.amazon.com/Becoming-Amish-Romance-Paige-Millikin-ebook/dp/B01MV3SBBQ.

Paige Millikin

ABOUT THE AUTHOR

Paige Millikin

Paige grew up in a small town outside of an Amish community in Ohio. After deciding she had enough winter to last a lifetime, Paige now resides in Florida where she enjoys the sunshine year round. If not in her writing room, you will find Paige running after her two children or trying to find time to have a date night with her husband.

With her own Christian upbringing a major influence in her life, Paige started writing clean, inspirational romances at an early age. She enjoys writing sweet wholesome stories, especially in the Amish and historical genre, that show the beauty of love and how special relationships are meant to be.

Find out more at https://www.amazon.com/-/e/B01MXKAEA3

If you would like to be notified of new (and free) books by Paige Millikin, you can sign up for a newsletter here.

Paige Millikin

You can reach Paige at:

mailto:PaigeMillikin@outlook.com

Twitter: https://twitter.com/PaigeMillikin

Facebook: https://www.facebook.com/PaigeMillikin

Paige Millikin

OTHER BOOKS BY PAIGE MILLIKIN

Paige is the author of the Plain & Simple Romance Series, a short series following a couple who did not expect to be together.

Plain & Simple: An Amish Romance

Plain & Simple 2: An Amish Courtship

Plain & Simple 3: An Amish Wedding

For a better value, get the set:

Plain & Simple: The Complete Collection

Becoming Amish is an Amish romance where Beth, a woman living on the outskirts of an Amish community, suffers a tragedy and is taken in by an Amish family. Will the way of the Amish pull her into the community or will the temptations of her English life be too much for her to leave?

Second Chances: Life Outside Amish Country is a short story following a woman who is doubting her decision to leave the community. After a chance encounter with a man on rumspringa, will she follow her heart back to her homestead or stay in the city that had captured her desires?

Mending the Heart is an Amish short story of Miriam and Kyle. After Kyle ends their courtship, he goes missing. Will his best friend Jacob and Miriam uncover the mystery and if so, how will they deal with what they find?

Don't Give Up on Me is a full length sweet romance novel set in a small town in Colorado where a woman is trying to pick up the pieces and decide to trust herself in another relationship. Will the spirit of Christmas thaw her skeptical heart?

Twinkling Lights: An Amish Christmas Romance follows an Amish woman who has always put her family first. When she decides to set out on a late rumspringa to find someone to settle down with, she meets her fair share of drama and Christmas miracles.

The Twelve Letters of Christmas is a shorter Regency Romance set in the 12 days before Christmas. A man with a tragic past that makes him loathe the holidays is given a task per day to help him reclaim the joy of Christmas.

The Lord's Country Estate Party is a Regency Romance set in the country estate of a Lord who falls in love with a guest at his party. However, another Lady has ill will towards the new couple and sets out to destroy them.

Murder Outside Amish Country Jonathan feels the call of *rumspringa*, despite his feelings for Miriam. He goes to the city and stays with a young man who had left the Amish community for good. The longer Jonathan stays, the more he doubts the *English* way of life is for him. But when he gets wrapped up in a murder investigation, he is certain that he belongs with the Amish.

Manufactured by Amazon.ca
Bolton, ON